Title: Third's Time the Charm
Subtitle: FFM Menage and Werewolf Shifter Romance Story

AF490522

From the Author:
Thank you for purchasing this book.

Table of Contents

Kathy Griffin loves working at the public relations company she has been working for in the past three years. However, when she was promoted to the assistant manager position and she had to work closely with the CEO, Amelia Tuffin, her work didn't seem as fun as before.

Amelia Tuffin is a cold-faced woman and hardly talks about herself. When Kathy realizes that she has a little crush on Amelia, she questions herself.

Axel Astor is a popular actor and signs a contract with Amelia's public relations team. He can't help but be drawn to the fierce but beautiful Amelia and wonders what secret she's carrying?

He finds himself cautious of Kathy when she is close to discovering the secret he harbors but questions himself when he begins to fall for her.

How will they be able to make that decision?

Chapter 1

Kathy Griffin smiled politely at her coworkers as she walked to the cubicle. The room housed ten of them, and although it was large, Kathy wished there were more space between herself and the other employees. Well, at least she could make the tiny cubicle her place. She did spend a lot of time there, working at her desk, and despite the workload, she was always bored. She found that incredible, though, that she had the ability to still search for some form of entertainment even though she barely had enough time on her hands.

Kathy shook the thoughts off and settled in her seat. Her long-time friend, Anna, smiled as soon as she saw her. They both worked at the company, with Anna joining a year after Kathy had. While Kathy wanted to say they had bonded immediately, it wasn't true.

She had judged her wrongly. Anna had walked up to her one day in the bathroom when she was bawling her eyes out for some reason. Ever since then, they had stuck close to each other.

"Hey, you." Anna held out a cup of coffee, and Kathy looked at her appreciatively.

"Hi, what's up?"

Anna shrugged and turned on the desktop. Although she was bubbly and more outgoing, she took her job seriously and always tried to make sure she did all her tasks. "Need to get the brief over with." Then, her face lit up. "Ooh, I heard something."

Kathy sat down and set up her table. She pushed her short hair behind her ears. She had always kept her hair short because it was low maintenance for her that way, but it had been growing, and she didn't have the time for a haircut. "What's that?"

"I heard that Axel Astor is about to be a client with us. That's so crazy!"

Kathy could faintly remember seeing a good-looking man having a press conference about some scandal on television. "Huh, I suppose."

Anna gaped. "Huh?? Really? *THE* Axel Astor is coming to partner with us, which is all you can see. Oh my God, nothing excites you."

Kathy shrugged and opened up a document on her laptop. She had a proposal to print and run by their boss.

Thankfully, Anna decided to stay quiet and focused on her work. The workspace began filling up, and people muttered their hellos. There were days like this. All people wanted to do was sit at their desks and mind their own business. There were also days when they chattered with each other and laughed at funny clients and their weird habits and behaviors.

Kathy gathered the printed papers and put them together in a file. She inhaled a fresh breath of air and stood up from her chair. Her boss unnerved her. It could be because there was always a permanent scowl on Ms. Amelia Tiffin's face. The older woman was probably one of the most beautiful women Kathy had seen, but for some reason, she never smiled.

Kathy wondered why. She owned an entire public relations agency and had such a nice car. Plus, she could nail anybody she wanted, but Kathy hadn't seen her with anyone. At least publicly.

Kathy shook off the thoughts and walked toward the office at the end of the corridor. She politely greeted people as they walked in and out of their offices, but everybody seemed busy. It looked like this Axel of a person was going to be such a demanding person.

Lucy, Amelia's receptionist, raised her eyebrows at her. As fitting, even her receptionist wasn't so friendly either.

Kathy cleared her throat. "Um, hi, I'm here to give Ms. Tiffin the proposal she had asked for."

Lucy barely looked at her. "Drop it here."

Kathy felt her cheeks color. She scrambled to drop the file on the table and then stopped. She had been asked to give Amelia, not Lucy. So why should she drop it? "Actually, I'd rather give Ms. Tiffin it myself."

Lucy stared at her, but Kathy refused to break her resolve. Finally, Lucy raised the phone to her ears and said some things before sending Kathy in.

"Thanks," Kathy said, which was met by a grunt.

She had been in Ms. Amelia's office once, and it still left her in awe of how large it was. What could one person do with all that space? Her entire living room could fit into a corner.

There was a glass wall that overlooked the tall buildings and busy streets of California. Amelia stood in front of it, staring down at the world. Just like she always did.

She turned around when Kathy walked in and barely looked at her. She held out a hand, requesting the document.

Kathy hurriedly gave it to her and stood. Amelia didn't ask her to sit either.

The silence seemed to thicken as Amelia flipped through the proposal, and Kathy felt sweat gather on her forehead. She tried to swallow the lump in their throat and prayed her hands stopped shaking.

Finally, Amelia spoke. "You did this yourself?"

She said it in a tone that gave the sense that she wouldn't appreciate it if Kathy were lying.

"Y-yes. I did."

Amelia nodded and reclined in her chair. She fixed her green eyes on Kathy, and Kathy swallowed, looking everywhere else but her.

"I see. Very well, come work with me."

Kathy felt the lump in her throat grow in size. She laughed nervously. "Well, I do work with you. I'm in the communications department and—"

Amelia cut her short with a wave of her hand. "I mean to work here as my executive assistant. I have been looking for one now, and I believe you can do the job. Judging from the proposal you wrote."

Kathy opened and closed her mouth. She wasn't sure what to say.

Amelia rolled her eyes and stood up. She was a tall woman with such a fit and amazing body that Kathy couldn't stop staring. Her blonde hair was styled in an expensive haircut. "I'll triple your salary, and you travel with me. I don't see how that's better than anything else."

Kathy decided to ignore how arrogant she sounded, and soon enough, she found herself nodding.

Amelia sat back in her chair. "Great. I'll have human resources prepare the contract. You start immediately."

Just like that, Kathy was dismissed. She stumbled out of the office in a daze. She took a quick trip to the bathroom and stared at herself in the mirror. She wished she had worn a better-looking outfit. She was in a white shirt, paired with gray slacks and a patterned vest. It looked so bland compared to the exquisite cream dress Amelia wore.

Kathy walked out of the bathroom and back to her office.

Anna looked at her inquisitively. "You look so dazed. Why?"

Kathy sat down and looked around. She didn't want other people eavesdropping. "I just got promoted."

Anna was confused. "Huh?"

Kathy quickly summarized the ordeal with Amelia and watched as Anna's eyes bulged.

"Oh my gosh, that's awesome. But why are we whispering?" Anna asked in an excited whisper.

"Because I don't want anyone to know about it yet. At least, until it's official."

Anna pouted. "But I'll miss you here."

"I'll miss you too. Don't worry, we'll always catch up outside of work."

Anna hugged her friend and got back to work. Kathy tried to work, but she couldn't concentrate properly. All she could wonder was what it would be like working closely with the *infamous* Ms. Tiffin.

Chapter 2

Kathy looked herself up and down in the mirror one more time. It was her first official day as Amelia's executive assistant, and she wanted to look the part. She had bought a dark purple dress that hugged her slim figure and, at least, made her look more official than she usually did. She had paired the dress with some dark pumps and hoped that she would be able to make the day with them.

Kathy had even tried applying some foundation and mascara, which was good enough. She had never been a huge fan of makeup, simply because she didn't know how to do it.

Her home was a quaint little thing, but it was her comfort zone. It had one bedroom and a living room, and since she was the only one in it, it was good enough for her.

Kathy grabbed her essentials, such as her phone, a new notebook, a pen and the other things she usually carried to work. Amelia hadn't told her what she needed to bring, but human resources had briefed her on her new role's expectations.

Kathy let out a huge breath as she locked the door behind her. She made her way to the large parking lot and spotted her eggplant-colored Volkswagen Beetle. Now that she could afford it, she hoped to change her car soon, but she also wondered if that was a good investment since she would be spending a lot of time traveling with Amelia.

Kathy glanced at the time. She would be early, but she better get on the road already. She drove her car out of the parking lot and made her way onto the busy roads of California.

There was a bit of traffic, and Kathy glanced up to see a large billboard of Axel Astor. It was for some lotion brand,

and she couldn't help but wonder why he looked that way. Like a carved statue. Beautiful, but somewhat lifeless.

Since Anna wouldn't stop mentioning him, Kathy finally searched up his name, and there were quite some tasteful articles about him. Turned out she was right, and he did have a scandal. He had managed to beat up some poor guy on some drunken night at the bar.

She wasn't patient enough to see why the altercation had occurred, but she knew it didn't look good for him. Kathy knew that was why he wanted to partner with their agency. To clean up his mess.

She scoffed and drove off as the traffic eased. Just in time, she pulled into the parking lot of the office building at the same time that Amelia did.

She was wearing dark pants with a light blue blouse. Kathy's dismay, she was wearing a white sweater vest which she managed to pull off. Kathy wondered why she had never looked that good in a sweater vest.

Kathy scrambled out of the car and walked up to her. "Good morning, ma'am."

"I expect you to get to the office before me. Don't let it happen again."

"Of course. Never again." Kathy bit her lip as she walked behind her. "This morning, by 8:30 am, you have a meeting with some L'Oréal executives. They want to discuss strengthening their publicity in Africa."

Amelia nodded as she pushed open the door to her office. Lucy stood up to greet her and narrowed her eyes at Kathy. Kathy chose to ignore her and followed Amelia into the office.

"Great. You'll be there for the meeting. Jot down the important points."

Kathy nodded, then realized the woman wasn't looking at her before saying a yes. "By nine o'clock, Axel Astor will be here."

Amelia sat at her desk and frowned. It was just like she was trying to place the name. "Ah, the actor. Of course. I suppose I'll have to see him myself. This is one of our biggest clients, and I can't afford to let some newbie ruin things. Remind me."

"Yes, ma'am." Kathy ran through the rest of the schedule and wondered how Amelia was going to keep up. She wondered for herself also. She was going to be there for most, if not all, the meetings, and it seemed like it was going to be a busy day.

"Until a permanent office is etched out for you, you'll have to make do with the corner over there." Amelia pointed a perfectly manicured finger at a single desk and chair set in the corner.

Kathy walked up to the desk, which was devoid of anything except a laptop and settled right in. She wished she had her personal space, but at least it was far away from Amelia. The woman was starting to unnerve her, and Kathy was afraid of saying the wrong things.

Before she realized, it was already time to meet with the L'Oréal's executives. Working at the ompany for three years, Kathy had had her fair share of meeting with celebrities, but she hadn't really been at such exclusive meetings before. She usually worked on the backend.

Well, polished people with thick, foreign accents soon settled themselves around the table in the conference room, and the meeting began.

Kathy watched in wonder as Amelia took hold of the meeting and commanded the room. She was able to make her client's wishes come through and stood her ground. It was amazing, and Kathy found herself to be in awe. She wrote down the details she felt were most important, and although she wished she were somewhere else, she plastered a smile on her face and nodded her head when it seemed appropriate.

Thankfully, the meeting ended, and they exited the room.

"I need you to go get Axel Astor from his house," Amelia said as she walked down the corridor.

Kathy was taken by surprise. Why should she pick a grown man from his home? Surely, this place wasn't difficult to navigate. Still, she couldn't argue. "Of course, ma'am."

"My driver will take you. The address has been sent to him. But he must come back to me immediately so that you'll get a ride with Axel. You have to leave now." Amelia walked into her office, leaving Kathy standing outside.

She blinked and began the walk to the lobby. Thankfully, Amelia's driver was sitting in a chair and stood up as soon as he spotted her.

They got into the car, and Kathy resisted the urge to sink into the soft seat. They made their way to the posh area of the city. Kathy couldn't help but notice how similar all the houses were. It would be very easy to go astray in that kind of place.

The driver dropped her in front of a huge mansion and drove off. Kathy huffed and hopped to God that the man was at least home.

She walked up to the door and pushed the doorbell. Soon enough, she heard some footsteps defending the stairs, and a slim brunette wrapped in a sheer robe opened the door. She raised a perfectly arched eyebrow at Kathy.

Kathy found herself stuttering at the woman's boobs seemed to stare at her in the face. Finally, she gained her composure. "Hi, I'm from Tiffin's agency, and I'm here for Mr. Astor."

The brunette smiled, seemingly unharmed. "Oh, I'm Tiffany. Come in." I'll go tell him." The woman sashayed up the stairs, and Kathy was left alone.

She opened her mouth as she took in her surroundings. Everything screamed expensive. There was a large painting hanging above the fireplace, and Kathy wondered if that was such a wise decision.

The furniture looked like it could pass as a marshmallow, and there was a shining oak coffee table right in the middle. Medals and plagues lined a shelf right beside the door, and Kathy knew that there was a reason it was the first thing one saw as soon as they entered the house.

"Damn. This is crazy, Kathy muttered to herself as she stared at the bear head rug. She hoped it was at least faux fur.

Kathy heard footsteps coming down the stairs and turned to see whether it was Tiffany bearing news. However, it was Axel Astor, coming down the stairs in all his glory.

Kathy felt the air leave her body. She had seen pictures of Axel, but mostly at face level. None of them could do justice to what she was seeing now.

He had a towel wrapped around his waist as water dripped down his body. He shook his head, and water droplets flew from his dark hair. Kathy stared at his lips as the moisture made them look even plumper.

She swallowed and tried not to look at the towel, dangerously getting lower.

Axel held out his hand. "Hi, I'm Axel. I'm sorry, I'm getting ready. You can make yourself comfy, and I'll be done in a jiffy."

Kathy could only swallow and nod. Tiffany climbed down the stairs and put an arm around Axel's neck.

He looked genuinely surprised to see her. "Brittany? What are you doing here."

Kathy looked somewhere else as Tiffany's jaw slacked open. "It's Tiffany, you ass." She ran up the stairs and gathered her clothes. As soon as she came down, she smacked Axel soundly on his cheeks and walked out of the house in a huff.

The silence between Kathy and Axel stretched, and Kathy wondered who was more stunned. She or him. "Um, I'll just wait here." She quickly sat on the couch and looked away from him. Her cheeks burned with embarrassment for him. "

"Yeah. I'll be back." Axel walked up the stairs slowly, as if he couldn't believe what had happened to him.

Kathy bit her lip and glanced to make sure he was gone before she snickered to herself. It's not every day you see a famous actor getting smacked right in the face. She couldn't wait to tell Anna what had happened.

Thankfully, Axel was back in some jeans and a t-shirt in record time. "Come on, let's go," he said to Kathy, beckoning for her to follow him.

They made their way to his garage, and Kathy felt her mouth open as the automatic door did open, revealing the wide array of sports cars.

Axel grinned at her reaction and pointed the key at a dark red Ferrari. "I'll be taking that today."

He drove the car out, and Kathy opened the door to get in. With that, they sped away.

Chapter 3

The journey back to the office was quicker than she had expected, and Kathy was thankful for it. Axel was a wild driver, and she felt her nails digging into her seat each time she heard the car roar louder. Still, she didn't complain and let out a breath of relief when she saw their company insight.

"This way," Kathy said as she led him up the stairs to Amelia's office. He had worn a baseball hat and some glasses in an attempt to disguise. Luckily for him, everyone at the office seemed too busy to take a closer look at him.

Kathy knocked on Amelia's office door and stepped in when she heard the woman ask her to go on.

Amelia stood up with a smile. "Axel. It's lovely to see you."

Axel stepped into the room and kissed her on the cheek. "I must say the same. You look quite different from what I had expected. In a good way."

Amelia smiled politely. It wasn't the first time she had heard such a compliment.

Kathy stared at the two of them. Although it seemed like this was their first-time meeting, she could have sworn that a flash of familiarity went between them. She shook it off and proceeded to leave the room.

"Oh no. Stay." Amelia pointed at Kathy.

They all settled on a couch as Lucy poured steaming coffee for them. Kathy inhaled the rich smell and sipped the piping hot beverage.

"So, I have run through your file, and your agent has spoken to me about the entire issue, but I wanted to hear from you. So tell me. What would you like us to do for you?"

"I mean, I just want the whole issue to die down. And I want to be the most polished version of myself."

Amelia nodded. "You do realize that you also have a huge role to play. You need to be on your best behavior."

Axel straightened and nodded. "I understand. I will be."

They spoke for some time, and Kathy tried to write all she could write down, but she got distracted staring at Axel. His face was something to behold. It was smooth, yet the jarring lines of his jaw gave him a rugged look.

He had well-toned arms, and she wondered how much he had to work for them. Kathy had noticed a thick scar on his neck and wondered where he had gotten such a puckering scar. It seemed like the only flaw in his otherwise perfect exterior.

Thankfully, the meeting ended, and Axel stood up. "You'll be seeing a lot of me."

Kathy didn't know if he directed the comment to her or Amelia, but he was looking at her, so she nodded. "Of course. I look forward to that."

Amelia walked him out, and Kathy remained in the office. Her stomach rumbled, and she became aware she hadn't eaten anything all morning. She bit her lips and held her stomach. She had developed an ulcer earlier and could feel the pain in her belly increase.

When Amelia walked back into the office, Kathy tried to hide the discomfort on her face, but her boss had already narrowed her eyes at her. "What's the problem?"

"Oh, nothing." Kathy's voice sounded strangled. She could have been able to get away with it, but her belly decided to let out a loud growl.

Amelia lifted a brow and grabbed her purse. "Why don't we grab lunch together? We can go to my spot. We can't have you fall over and collapse now, can we?"

Kathy opened her mouth to argue. She decided that it wouldn't be wise. She nodded and followed Amelia as they walked out of the office.

They didn't have to drive too far at all. As soon enough, the car was parked right in front of a five-star restaurant.

Kathy had expected to go to the local sandwich shop, not this high end-looking place.

The host smiled at Amelia and greeted her with reverence. He led them to a private booth and settled down.

"I'll have the lamb chops and rice, please," Amelia said to the waiter.

"I'll have the same too," Kathy said when the waiter turned to take her order.

There would have been an awkward silence if not for the soft music playing in the background, at least from Kathy's side.

It was weird for her, sitting at some nice restaurant with her boss whom she hadn't said more than five words before the present week.

She was grateful when they brought their meal. At least, that was something for her to focus on.

"You shouldn't skip breakfast," Amelia said with a frown.

"I just wanted to make it in time."

"It's no good if you have an issue at work." Amelia looked at her for a while before settling with her food.

They ate quietly, with Kathy scanning the restaurant with her eyes as they ate. It was nice, for a change, to be somewhere like that.

"We have a fundraising event to attend this weekend. You will be accompanying me."

It was not a question, and Kathy could only not in response to Amelia's statement. "Of course. That's no problem."

***

Anna scrunched up her nose and shook her head. "Yeah, this won't work. You need a better outfit."

Kathy was panicking, and she groaned. "Oh gosh, this is my last formal dress. I don't have anything else."

Anna put a hand on her hips. "How come you're telling me now? We could have gotten something during the week. Now the day is here."

"I thought I had something to wear. I was so sure I had something to wear."

"Well, now you don't."

Kathy sank to her bed miserably. She wished she could cancel but she knew Amelia would have her head. She couldn't dare.

There was a thud at the door, and Anna raised her brows. "Are you expecting someone?" she asked.

Kathy shook her head and stood up. She walked toward the door and looked into the peephole. There was a man in a uniform, holding something that looked like a box.

She opened the door carefully. "May I help you?"

"Delivery for a Miss Kathy Griffin?"

"That's me."

"Okay. Please sign here. And here."

Kathy signed and collected the box. She shut the door behind her and walked toward a very curious Anna.

"Ooh, what is that?"

Inquisitively, Kathy gently opened the box and gasped when she saw the content.

"Oh my gosh," Anna's eyes widened.

Kathy brought out a light pink dress that sparkled faintly under the light. There was an open back, and the neckline plunged a little.

Also in the box were some black heels and a black suede purse.

"Scandalous. I love it." Anna nodded as she held up the dress.

Kathy noticed that there was a small note in the box. *I assume you don't have a dress.*

Yep. Definitely sounded like her.

Chapter 4

Kathy was supposed to drive to meet Amelia at her home, and if she was honest, she was a little curious to see where her boss lived.

Amelia's home was all alone in its surroundings. Kathy shivered as she drove up to the large house. She wondered how the woman lived all by herself in such a large house in the middle of nowhere.

Kathy got out of her car and rang the bell.

"Coming," A cheerful voice rang out, and an older woman opened the door.

She wore cleaning attire and was holding a vacuum cleaner in her hand. "Ah, you must be Kathy. Come in, come in. Ms. Tiffin said you should wait for her in the living room."

Kathy nodded and stepped into the room. She wobbled a bit in her heels but soon gained balance. Her cheeks reddened when she saw that the cleaner had seen her falter.

She sat gingerly on a dark red leather couch and folded her arms, waiting. She had expected the house to be devoid of character and completely bare, but Kathy was surprised to see the hints of personality around the house.

There were photo frames from the various stages of Amelia's life, and Kathy smiled when she saw a very chubby prepubescent Amelia. She couldn't imagine the woman to be less perfect than ever.

There was a snow globe on the mantle, and Kathy stood up and walked toward it.

Right in the middle of the globe was a caricature of Amelia in a snowy town. Kathy shook it and giggled as the caricature tumbled alongside Emilia.

"A friend in London gave it to me." Kathy was startled by the sudden voice and quickly dropped the globe before turning around. "I'm sorry." She started, but her voice faded away.

Amelia wore a black dress that flowed out around her waist. There was a single strap, and it showed off her toned skin. Her hair had been curled around her face, and there was bright red lipstick on her lips.

Kathy's heart thumped, and she was afraid that Amelia would hear her. She was fierce and beautiful all at the same time.

Amelia nodded her head approvingly. "The dress suits you. Hold on."

She walked to Kathy and turned Kathy around as she adjusted the cloth. Kathy closed her eyes and inhaled her perfume. It smelled like blackberries and seduction.

What was wrong with her? She couldn't possibly be attracted to her boss.

Her skin sizzled when Amelia had touched her, even after the woman stepped away.

"We need to leave," Amelia said and walked away from her.

Kathy followed her behind as they got into the car.

Nicholas, who was Amelia's driver, as Kathy had learned, greeted them and soon, they were on their way.

Kathy fixed her gaze on the view outside the car, and she tried not to acknowledge the presence of Amelia. On the other hand, her budding feelings.

She couldn't believe that was happening to her. She didn't want to feel that way for her boss. Not when she was so closed off and cold to the people around her.

Thankfully, Amelia didn't say much other than to prep her on the type of people they would converse with at the party. Clients.

They got to the venue, and Kathy was in awe of how large it was. Lights were on every corner, and even the parking lot was lit up.

Various scents of perfumes filled the parking lot as people got out from their luxurious cars in luxurious dresses.

Kathy followed Amelia, and she blushed as men stared at her, impressed. Even though she was attracted to both men and women, she didn't get much attention from either, which was all new to her.

They put some identifying wristbands around their hands and went into the venue.

Violin music played as they entered the event center, and tables were arranged in each corner of the hall with numbers on them.

Kathy glanced at her wristband. They were placed at number seven.

"Oh, great," Amelia muttered under her breath as she spotted the table.

Kathy followed her gaze and looked at the two women already at the table. They seemed to have spotted Amelia and were muttering behind their hands. She wondered who they were.

With a confident stride, Amelia walked up to the table.

One of the two women, dressed in a hot pink gown, smiled at Amelia. "Oh, what a surprise to see you here. We thought you would never attend public events again."

Kathy tried to keep her face neutral, but she wondered what the woman was on about.

"Lisa," Amelia said in a tone that could pass as a warning or a greeting. "Joleen. It's nice to see you again."

Joleen smiled, but her face barely changed. Kathy suspected it was because of too much Botox, maybe. "Of course, darling. You look the same."

Kathy picked up on the hostility and sat gingerly in her seat. She wasn't sure what was going on but knew it would be best if she just stayed quiet.

Thankfully, the hall began filling up, and the woman got distracted as they made their comments on people's outfits.

"Hello, ladies." Kathy turned around at the sound of the voice. It was Axel, and he was wearing a gold-colored tux tailored specifically for him.

"Mr. Astor. It's quite astonishing to see you here." Amelia genuinely looked surprised. Kathy remembered that she had told him to stay out of public events in the meantime. Clearly, he didn't heed her words.

"Ah well, I can't help but be drawn to the public scene. Anyway, I'll see you two around. Kathy, you look lovely," Axel said before walking away.

Kathy felt her heart skip a beat as she watched his receding figure.

The hall filled up, and the event began. The host, an elderly woman who seemed quite delighted to be there, said something, but Kathy wasn't really listening. She was stunned by the number of famous people in the room. It was all new to her.

"So, is this your new eye candy? You haven't had any of those since you came out." Lisa threw a jab at Amelia. The table had been silent until the two women spoke, and Kathy was taken aback. She hadn't known about her boss's sexuality, but suddenly it made sense to her.

Amelia's face was blank, and she said in a quiet voice. "Please, excuse me." She stood up and left the room.

Kathy watched her receding figure and turned to face the two women. "I don't know who Ms. Amelia is to you, but she's a hard-working woman and is twice the person you are. Her sexuality doesn't concern you. You should be worried about your husbands, or lack of." With a huff, Kathy left the table.

Her heart was racing, and she couldn't believe she had said what she had said. There was no way that had come out of her mouth, but it had.

She strolled out of the building and rubbed her arms as the chilly cold hit her. It was midnight and much colder outside than it was inside.

Kathy looked around, but Amelia was nowhere to be found. She brought her phone to dial the number. It rang, but nobody picked.

Kathy turned to the back of the building and was nervous to see that the place was devoid of people.

"Amelia? Um, Miss Tiffin?" Kathy called out into the dark.

The bushes rustled, and she felt her heartbeat race faster. She took a step backward as the rustle became louder. A large black dog appeared from the bushes.

Kathy gasped at the size of the dog. It didn't look like a regular dog. Its fangs were much longer and looked more dangerous. Also, its fur was longer than a domestic dog. Kathy tried to convince herself otherwise, but something told her that she was looking at a real-life wolf.

It was bleeding from its side, and that was when Kathy ran away from the place.

Panting heavily, she ran up the stairs by the sides and pushed open a heavy door leading to the rooftop.

Standing all by herself was Amelia. She turned to look at who it was and seemed surprised to see Kathy.

"How did you find me?"

Kathy shook her head, struggling to catch her breath. "Honestly, I don't know."

Amelia frowned. "Are you all right?"

"Yes." Kathy straightened. "Just trying to catch my breath."

Amelia nodded and turned to stare at the view of the city. Everything was so high up from here, and Kathy didn't get as close to the balcony as Amelia was. She was a little scared of heights.

"You know, I came out only a few years ago. I was so scared it would be in the tabloids. Thankfully, nobody seemed to care much. Well, nobody except California's exclusives." Amelia spat the words out, irritated. "Quite embarrassing for them, hypocritical too. They are accepting of everyone except me. I haven't dated anyone since I divorced my ex-husband years ago."

Kathy was surprised by this news. She hadn't known Amelia had been married. Still, she kept quiet. She didn't want the woman to stop.

Amelia let out a laugh devoid of humor. "It doesn't matter how lonely it gets. I'd rather be all by myself than to be mocked."

Kathy felt her heartache for her. "It doesn't matter what they say. I think you are such a spectacular woman. If no one wants to be with you, it's simply because they aren't good enough."

Amelia laughed. "Oh, please. I'm not going to fire you if you;re honest."

Kathy took a step closer and looked at her. For the first time, she could see cracks in the armor that Amelia Tiffin had created. "I mean, you can be quite a meanie sometimes, and you aren't exactly the nicest person, but I think if you allow yourself, you could be the kindest person ever."

Amelia looked into her eyes as unshed tears glimmered in them. Kathy felt drawn to the older woman. It was like a spell that couldn't be broken.

"And I think you are the most attractive woman ever," Kathy whispered as she lifted a hand to wipe the tears in Amelia's eyes.

Slowly, Amelia closed her eyes and leaned in. She moved closer until her lips touched Kathy's. And sparks flew in the air as they kissed under the midnight sky.

Chapter 5

Kathy stalled outside the office building on shaky legs. She wasn't sure how she could face Amelia after what had happened between them, but she knew she had to.

She inhaled a deep breath and made her way into the building. Kathy greeted some workers on the way and was shocked when they responded to her. Usually, she was met with a grunt or a halfhearted hello.

Lucy still hadn't warmed up to her, but at least she wasn't given her death glares anymore.

Kathy knocked on the door and entered when Amelia told her to come in.

"Good morning," Kathy said, although she was surprised to see Axel sitting across from Amelia.

Amelia looked normal, and she put on a small smile. "Morning. Please sit." Then she addressed them both. "I must say, while I thought the public appearance was too soon, it did a little good for you, Axel. Let's keep it that way, fresh and clean."

Axel nodded, then winced.

Kathy looked at him with concern. "Are you okay?"

Axel nodded and gave a stiff smile. "Yeah. Just hurt my side a little, that's all. It's nothing."

Something pricked at the back of Kathy's mind, and she frowned, trying to place it. But she decided to let it go. "All right. Take it easy."

Amelia nodded in agreement. "Yeah, go to the hospital if it hurts."

Axel shook his head firmly. "Nah, it's just a small scratch."

"Well then," Amelia said. "Kathy, Axel has a promotional shoot today. Please accompany him. I want to ensure I don't miss out on all the details."

"All right, of course."

Axel stood up. "Well, I have to run some quick errands. Kathy, I'll be back here real soon."

Kathy nodded and smiled as he left the room. When the door was shut behind him, the room was smaller.

Kathy swallowed and looked everywhere else but at Amelia.

Amelia stood up and cleared her throat. "What happened on Saturday..."

Kathy bit her lip. "I am so sorry, ma'am. I promise it won't happen again."

Amelia raised a brow. "Really? You didn't like it?"

Kathy's face turned red." What? No, I did, but I just assumed... you didn't."

Amelia moved closer to Kathy and leaned on the table, right in front of her seat. Kathy could smell her perfume and see the star birthmark on her neck. She wanted to kiss it.

"Well, I did like it. Very much. Can I do it again?"

Kathy swallowed and nodded. She leaned in closer and allowed Amelia to take her lips in hers.

A moan escaped Kathy's lips as Amelia kissed her with an urgent fervency. They stood up at once and made their way to the couch.

Amelia leaned over Kathy and trailed kisses down her neck. Kathy felt like someone had set fire to her blood, and it was boiling. She couldn't get enough of it.

Amelia gently slipped a hand into Kathy's dress and traced lines over her thighs.

Feeling confident, Kathy moved Amelia's hands upward, looking into her eyes. Kathy put a hand inside Amelia's blouse and stroked her firm breasts.

Amelia began working her hands on Kathy's clit, looking into her eyes as Kathy grew breathless.

Kathy's gasp became fainter as Amelia worked her fingers faster and quietly; she orgasmed onto Amelia's hands.

Amelia chuckled and brought some tissue paper to clean up. "Well, how was that?"

Kathy swallowed and nodded. "Good. Really good."

Then Amelia kissed her on the cheek. "Anytime."

A loud bang came at the door, followed by Axel's voice. The two women scrambled to look normal, and Amelia told Axel to enter.

Axel lifted a brow at the tow of them standing stiffly. "Are you okay?"

"Yes, yes. You need to get going." Amelia said and went back to her desk.

Kathy nodded and followed Axel out the door, avoiding his curious gaze.

He had brought another car, but at least it was a normal-looking jeep. Kathy guessed he didn't really want to draw any attention to himself.

They got into the car and made their way onto the busy roads of California.

"So, do you want to say why your cheeks are so flushed?"

Kathy opened and closed her mouth before placing a hand on her cheek. "No, they're not. I'm fine, really,"

Axel shrugged. "All right then. Well, you are about to see me in my element, so you may be more flushed than this. Prepare yourself."

Kathy rolled her eyes at his smirk. "I'll be fine." She was a little curious to see what Axel was like in front of the camera.

They pulled up at some open set. There were cameras everywhere, and people were pacing all over the place.

Axel walked toward a woman, and Kathy followed him. She ignored the glances people gave her and tried to remain as professional as possible.

"Damien, this is Kathy. Kathy, this is Damien, the director."

Damien was a bald man with impeccable fashion taste and a bright smile to go with it. "Oh, lovely. My pleasure." Then he turned to Axel. "The shoot is about to begin. You need to get ready. Go to the dressing room. There are people there already."

Axel turned to Kathy and winked at her. "Want to come? It'll be fun."

Kathy ignored his suggestive tone and rolled her eyes. "No thanks."

Axel spoke. "Actually, I think it'll be nice for you to go with me. I heard you are supposed to take notes or something."

Kathy couldn't help but agree with him. "All right, Let's go."

They made their way to a trailer, and when Axel opened the door, Kathy could have easily mistaken the interior for a small house.

People rushed at Damien to take him to get ready. Kathy slowly followed them behind, taking in the room.

She wondered if this was a one-time something and if so, they had done a good job putting it together.

Axel sat in front of a mirror while a woman touched his face with some powder.

"So, you do this a lot?"

Axel looked at her in the mirror. "What? The shoots? Yeah. Before I became an actor, I was a model."

Kathy nodded. It did make sense. He seemed to fit perfectly in the whole scene.

Kathy decided to go all out and asked, "So, why did you beat up a man?"

Axel pursed his lips and looked around. "I'll like to be alone for a few minutes. I'll be down soon." They had dressed him in simple outfits, but it only seemed to make him look even better.

Soon enough, the trailer was empty except for them. Axel turned around to look at her. "The truth?"

Kathy nodded.

"Well, I beat him up because he kept calling this woman a whore, since she wouldn't give him her number. It was all ridiculous to me."

"Why didn't you ever say that was why?"

Axel laughed. "When you are a public figure like me, nothing is ever good enough. It didn't matter the story I told. The tabloids already decided the story to publish."

Kathy stared at him for a moment. She felt bad that he had to be in that type of position, not to be able to defend his name.

Axel winced and held his side. Kathy frowned and walked up to him. "What's the problem?"

Axel shook his head. "It's nothing really."

Kathy narrowed her eyes and pulled his hands off his side. She slowly lifted his shirt and stared in horror at what was right before her. There was a blood-soaked bandage wrapped around him, and Kathy unwrapped it to reveal a deep wound.

"What the hell?" she swore.

Axel tried to hide it from her. "It's nothing. I just fell."

Kathy scoffed. "Fell my ass. That doesn't look like a wound you get from falling."

Axel looked away. "Just leave it."

Kathy had the sense that he didn't want to talk about it. So she decided to let the issue go. "But I'm going to have to redress that. Or you go to the hospital."

Axel shook his head. "No, I'm not going to the hospital. You can redress it, thanks."

Kathy crossed her fingers and hoped that there was a first aid box somewhere around. Thankfully, she found a box in a cabinet and took some gauze, a fresh set of bandages and some balm to ease the sting.

She cleaned the wound as gently as she could because she knew it had to hurt a lot. When it looked like it wouldn't develop any infection, she wrapped it in the bandage.

"All done. After this, you need to go home and rest as much as you can. Really."

Axel grinned. "Geez, you sound like my mom. Yeah yeah, I will. Thanks again."

A knock on the trailer door signified that it was time for the shoot to begin.

Axel exited the room, and Kathy trailed behind him.

She sat in a corner as they offered her some iced tea while she watched Axel pose for the camera. He was a natural and worked perfectly well with the director, so much that they were in sync.

Kathy sipped her tea and blushed as she remembered her moment with Amelia. She wasn't sure what was going on between them. She wished they could come out and say what it really was, but Kathy was too scared to make the first move. It hurt her that there was the possibility it could be something very casual for Amelia. She didn't want to think much about it and brought out her notebook to write all there was to write.

Thankfully, the shoot didn't take too long, and Axel shook hands with the director before going to meet Kathy.

"Hey, you."

"Hey."

"Want to grab lunch?"

Kathy was taken aback by how offhandedly Axel said it, but she nodded in response. She was quite hungry and made a mental note to stop skipping breakfast.

They hopped into Axel's car, and he drove them to some takeout restaurant, where they ordered cheeseburgers.

Kathy admitted that she was a little surprised he could order something as normal as that. "So where are we going?"

Axel smirked. "I want to take you to my spot."

Kathy laughed. "You have a spot? Well, let's see where it is."

They drove for a little while and finally rounded into an open field.

There was a wooden cart in the corner, and it had a covering that shielded them from the sun. There were packed sacks in the cart to soften the seat, and the two made themselves comfortable.

It was quite nice for Kathy to rest in a field of daffodils.

"It's so peaceful here."

Axel nodded as he closed his eyes. "Yeah, it is. I come here sometimes to get away from the buzz of it all."

Kathy nodded. "Yeah, I understand."

They fell into a comfortable silence before Axel finally spoke again. "So, tell me. How can I get Amelia to fall in love with me?"

Kathy barked out a surprised laugh. "Are you serious?"

Axel laughed also. "Well, half-serious. Maybe not love, but damn she is one fine woman."

Kathy smiled and nodded. "She is." Surprisingly, she didn't feel as jealous as she thought. She assumed it had to do with the fact that Amelia wasn't attracted to men.

Kathy turned to look at Axel and was surprised to see him watching her. "What?"

Axel smiled softly. "Nothing. You're quite an attractive woman yourself."

Kathy huffed. "Ha-ha, not really."

"No, really. You have these gorgeous large eyes that make you look so innocent."

Kathy looked at him. "Thank you."

Axel moved closer to her. Close enough that she could see the tiny bump on his nose, and she didn't fight it when he finally kissed her.

The kiss was long, slow and sweet. But Kathy knew that it was different from what she had felt with Amelia. Kissing Amelia was like loading herself with an explosion.

Finally, they separated, and Axel smiled. "I want to invite you and Amelia for dinner tonight."

Kathy lifted a brow. "You'll have to do that yourself."

All right. Let's go." Axel held out a hand to Kathy, and they made their way back to the car.

The drive back to the office wasn't awkward at all. If anything, Kathy felt like Axel was an old friend. They sang to the popular songs on the radio as they drove.

They pulled up to the office, chattering like old friends. They ran into Anna on the way, who was gaping like a fish when she saw Axel.

Kathy decided to take the chance. "Oh Axel, this is my best friend, Anna. Anna, this is—"

"Axel Astor. Heck, I know. It's nice to meet you. So nice." Kathy held out a hand to shake him.

Instead, Axel took the hand to his lips and kissed it gently. Kathy snickered quietly when she saw Anna's eyes bulged. Well, at least her friend had a story to tell everyone. They waved goodbye and continued on their way to the office.

Amelia wasn't surprised to see them, but she smiled when they came into her office. "You're back. How was it?"

"He is a natural." Kathy smiled and dropped the note in front of Amelia.

"You flatter me. Anyway, I was hoping I could invite you to dinner this evening. I'll cook. It's just a way of me showing my appreciation."

Amelia frowned. "Oh, Mr. Astor, if anything, we should be the ones thanking you."

Axel shook his head. "Of course not. I insist. And please, call me Axel."

Amelia pondered for a bit, and slowly, she nodded. "All right. What time?"

"Seven o'clock. I'll be sending the address to you."

They said their goodbyes, and Axel excused himself, saying he had a yoga appointment.

When they were left alone, Amelia stood up and grinned mischievously. "So, where were we?"

And after that, she pleased Kathy all over again.

Chapter 6

Kathy held onto Amelia's hands as Nicholas drove them to Axel's home. Amelia smiled back at her and squeezed her hand.

Kathy was a little disappointed when she released her hand as soon as they pulled up in front of Axel's house. But she didn't let that trouble her too much.

They walked toward the front door, and Axel opened the door after they rang the bell.

"Hey! You're here." He was wearing a shirt, and some slacks with the first two buttons of the shirt popped open.

Kathy had worn a dress with ruffled and was glad when Amelia said it was pretty. The older woman had worn a jumpsuit with pumps. Casual, but quite fitting for her.

"We brought wine." Amelia held up a bottle of expensive wine.

Axel grinned and collected the bottle. "Come right in."

They made their way to the dining table, where it had been set already, and there were candles lit around.

They were alone in the house, and Axel put on some soft music in the background.

They laughed as he served them the meal he had cooked. Kathy was surprised that the food was quite good and even decided to go for a second round.

She was glad to see that Amelia was smiling and seemed quite loosened up that night. It was something she didn't get to see quite often, and she thanked Axel mentally for the opportunity.

"Come on, drink some more." Kathy laughed as she topped Amelia's cup with more wine. She admitted she was a little tipsy, but Kathy was also glad for the alcohol in her system. It made her a little bold.

Many more glasses in, the three of them were giggling and staggering as the alcohol kicked into their system.

They made their way to the living room and tried to focus on the program showing.

Amelia looked at Kathy with want and began kissing her, ignoring Axel's presence.

Axel whistled. "Wow. Who knew you guys were together? This is hot."

Kathy giggled as Amelia kissed her.

Axel shook his head. "Man, can I join you guys?"

Amelia turned her head to him. "Do you want to?"

"Hell yeah."

Amelia turned to look at Kathy to see if it was okay with her. Kathy nodded as she stared at Axel with lust. She admitted she didn't like him as she did for Amelia, but she was attracted to him.

"Fuck yes." Axel stood up from his seat and made his way to them. He trailed kisses down Kathy's neck, and Amelia kissed her lips.

Kathy moaned at the sensation and knew that was an invitation for them.

Amelia reached into Kathy's dress, and Kathy massaged her breasts. Axel wasn't too behind either, and he gently grabbed Kathy's breasts and gave them a little squeeze.

"Let's go upstairs," Kathy whispered with want. They all followed Axel to his bedroom and were comforted that the bedroom was big enough for all of them.

Amelia pushed Kathy onto the bed and worked her mouth on Kathy's vagina. Kathy gasped as she kissed Axel and arched her back for him to grab her breasts.

"Can I?" Axel looked at the two women for permission. Both Kathy and Amelia nodded, and he grabbed a condom.

He wore it over his member and gently teased Kathy at her entrance. Amelia wasn't left behind as Kathy stroked her clit, looking into her eyes.

Slowly, Axel began moving into Kathy, falling into a rhythmic pulse. Kathy focused on pleasuring Amelia as the three of them were joined together by passion.

As they moved faster and moans escaped their lips, they rode on the wings of ecstasy as they came together.

***Kathy slowly opened her eyes and winced as the headache hit her. Memories of last night rushed through her head, and she blushed, remembering what had occurred between them. She liked it, though, and was glad she could bond more with Amelia.

Kathy glanced at the clock by the bed. It was a few minutes after two in the morning. Her throat felt like a desert, and she needed a cold glass of water.

She grabbed a robe and wrapped it around her body. Kathy looked around and realized that neither Axel nor Amelia were in the room.

She gently made her way down the stairs, just in case they were asleep somewhere else. Kathy heard some noise from the living room and stopped in her steps. Wondering what was happening.

She rounded the curve leading to the living room and gasped when she took in what was before her. The living room was completely upturned, and the furniture had been torn to pieces.

Kathy was frozen with fear when she saw something that threatened her sanity. Right in front of her were four large wolves, fighting with each other.

With a gasp, Kathy hit the floor with a loud noise, and everything went black.

***For the second time that day, Kathy's eyes fluttered open. She saw a very scared Amelia looking at her and a concerned Axel holding a glass of water for her.

Kathy groaned as she sat uprightly.

"No, no, just lie down." Amelia kissed her forehead and lowered her down onto the bed.

Memories of what she had seen rushed to Kathy, and she whimpered in fear. "I saw... I saw."

Axel held her hand. "Kathy, it's okay. We know."

Kathy frowned. "You know what?"

"That you saw wolves. Werewolves." Amelia bit her lip in guilt and stared at Kathy.

Kathy felt a sickening realization in her stomach. She curled into a ball and backed away from them. Her heart broke when Amelia's eyes welled up with tears, but her fear overshadowed everything. "Oh my gosh. This isn't real. Werewolves aren't real."

Axel was firm. "Kathy, listen. Could you allow us to explain? At least for your sanity."

Kathy opened her mouth to speak, but she decided to stay quiet.

Axel took the cue and spoke. "I'm a werewolf. There's no other way to say this, and so is Amelia. Before you say anything, we didn't know either of us were werewolves before we officially met. So this isn't some plan or game. Those other werewolves you saw were trying to attack us. I guess they smelled us out. We dealt with them, but not at a cost. The living room is in disarray, and my wound reopened. But it's nothing I can't fix."

Amelia held Kathy's quivering hands. "Kathy, I didn't mean to bring you into this. I didn't mean to fall for you. I wanted to keep that part of my life away from you because I was scared that you wouldn't be able to handle it. I'm scared that I'm right about that. I perfectly understand if you hate me and want me gone."

Kathy's teeth shook as she closed her eyes. Her lover was a werewolf. Or was it vixen? She didn't know. Kathy swallowed, and she looked into Amelia's eyes. She seemed genuine, and Kathy knew that the next words she spoke would determine everything else.

"Okay."

Amelia's face contorted with confusion. "Okay?"

"Okay. You are werewolves. Anything else I need to know?"

Axel smiled and shook his head. "Well, I have a double-jointed elbow, but that's all."

Kathy shook her head and looked at Amelia. "I'm going to be honest with you. This is still freaky for me, and it'll take some time for me to warm up to the idea, but I don't really care as long as it's still you, Amelia. I don't want anyone else, and your werewolf identify won't change that."

Tears dropped from Amelia's eyes as she hugged Kate tightly. "Oh, it's always been you."

Kathy turned to look at Axel. "So you were the wolf I saw? At the fundraising event?"

Axel nodded. Yep. "It was me. They attacked me at the event too."

Kathy nodded and turned to look at Amelia. She looked even more beautiful when she cried.

Axel quietly exited the room, leaving the two women alone.

Amelia gathered Kathy in her arms and hugged her to herself. "You know, I'm thirty-five. Is that too old for you?"

Kathy laughed. "You are only five years older than I am. Plus, I don't really care."

Amelia turned to look at her with a serious look on her face. "Will you be my woman? I've never uttered those words out loud, but I don't think I want to say that to anyone else but you."

Kathy bit her lip and slowly kissed Amelia on her lips. "Yes. Over and over again. I want to be."

"Good. So I can do this?" Amelia smiled mischievously as she lowered herself to Kathy's thighs. She slowly pulled apart the robe, revealing a very naked Kathy.

Kathy blushed with embarrassment but was soon gasping with pleasure as Amelia worked her tongue into her. She could get used to that.

Amelia gently played with her already hard nipples as Kathy came with a loud gasp.

"Well, I should return the favor," Kathy said as she gently pushed Amelia down.

She laughed at the surprised look on Amelia's face and pulled off her clothes. She sat on the older woman, making sure that their vagina lips were locked as she began to move on her.

Amelia moaned, and Kathy took that cue to quicken her pace. She knew that their moans were all over the place, but Kathy didn't care. All she wanted was that moment with Amelia, and as their bodies shook together, she knew she had it.

Interlocked, they lay on the bed, wrapped in each other's arms. Amelia turned to look at her. "I can't wait to show you to everyone. I want to be loud about you. None of that hiding thing."

Kathy smiled and kissed her lips. "I can't wait to show you off too. To tell everyone that you are mine."

And truly, she was.

THE END

www.ingramcontent.com/pod-product-compliance
Lightning Source LLC
Chambersburg PA
CBHW060921130726
48001CB00006B/2351